Welcome to the world of Beast Quest!

Tom was once an ordinary village boy, until he travelled to the City, met King Hugo and discovered his destiny. Now he is the Master of the Beasts, sworn to defend Avantia and its people against Evil. Tom draws on the might of the magical Golden Armour, and is protected by powerful tokens granted to him by the Good Beasts of Avantia. Together with his loyal companion Elenna, Tom is always ready to visit new lands and tackle the enemies of the realm.

While there's blood in his veins, Tom will never give up the Quest…

TO
AVANTIA

PORT
CALM

THE LOST
CITY OF VIGA

WOODS
WITHOUT
END

Mallix
THE SILENT STALKER

BY ADAM BLADE

With special thanks to Tabitha Jones

www.beastquest.co.uk

ORCHARD BOOKS

First published in Great Britain in 2021 by The Watts Publishing Group

1 3 5 7 9 10 8 6 4 2

Text © Beast Quest Limited 2021
Cover and inside illustrations by Steve Sims
© Beast Quest Limited 2021

Beast Quest is a registered trademark of Beast Quest Limited
Series created by Beast Quest Limited, London

A CIP catalogue record for this book is available from the British Library.

ISBN 978 1 40836 217 4

Printed in Great Britain

Orchard Books
An imprint of Hachette Children's Group
Part of The Watts Publishing Group Limited
Carmelite House, 50 Victoria Embankment, London EC4Y 0DZ

An Hachette UK Company
www.hachette.co.uk
www.hachettechildrens.co.uk

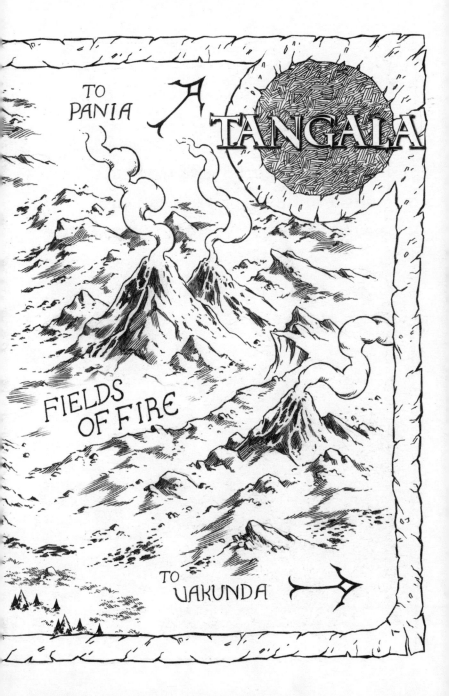

There are special gold coins to collect in this book. You will earn one coin for every chapter you read.

Find out what to do with your coins at the end of the book.

CONTENTS

It is always said that Tangala has no Beasts. That, I'm pleased to say, is not quite true. There are Beasts here – terrifying ones – but they are sleeping. I will awaken them. I will fill them with rage and evil. And I will set them loose on the people of this kingdom.

Vakunda was my prison, but now I'm free. They thought I was dead. They were wrong.

I have lived for five hundred years. I have vanquished any who stood in my path. No puny Avantian boy will stop me now. My Beasts will ravage and destroy Tangala and I will stand over the ruins, ruler of all.

Zargon

GHOST WARRIOR

Tom and Elenna stood side by side, high on a clifftop at the western shore of Tangala, gazing out over the moonlit sea. Tom felt gritty-eyed and bone tired after their recent battle with Teknos, a giant turtle-Beast. He took a deep breath, relishing the cool breeze on his skin.

Gentle waves rolled on to the

shadowy beach far below – the water calm again, now that Teknos had been returned to his resting place beneath the ocean. But still, dread gnawed at Tom's gut. Though he and Elenna had managed to save the nearby fishing village of Port Calm from Teknos's furious rampage, their Quest had only just begun.

Zargon, a powerful Evil Wizard, had stolen four ancient, magical weapons from the tombs below Queen Aroha's palace – each capable of awakening a mighty Beast. Crazed with revenge, Zargon would stop at nothing until he had brought the kingdom of Tangala to its knees.

"Not while there's blood in my veins," Tom vowed under his breath.

The problem was, they had no way of knowing where to head next. No map, no clues. Zargon could be awakening another Beast at that very moment, and they'd be powerless to prevent him.

A sudden gust of icy wind slammed into Tom from behind, almost pitching him and Elenna over the cliff. He caught his balance and grabbed Elenna's sleeve, pulling her back from the edge. They both turned and froze. The grass rippled silver in the moonlight and the dusky shadows swirled.

"What's that?" Elenna asked, her

voice tight with fear. In the darkness,
a huge pale shape coalesced before
them. Tom gasped as he made out
a woman standing tall on a chariot
pulled by two gleaming white horses,
their coats dappled with shifting
purples and greys. The woman's hair

and the manes of the horses eddied
gently around them as if underwater,
and Tom realised he could see the
stars through their ghostly forms. The
woman's face was pale, like marble,
and shimmered with a radiant light,
but her coal-dark eyes seemed to

bore into Tom's soul. Tom gripped the hilt of his sword as the woman raised a hand, palm forwards.

"I mean you no harm," she said, in a deep voice that penetrated the wind. In her other hand, she held a spear – an exact duplicate of the one Zargon had thrown into the ocean to awaken Teknos.

"Who are you?" Tom murmured – although in his heart, he knew she had to be the warrior who had first laid the turtle-Beast to rest, then perished, more than four hundred years ago.

"I am Celesta," the woman said. "I congratulate you both on your victory. Teknos sleeps once more, and for that, I am eternally grateful. But now a terrible Evil arises in the North. Even as we speak, a Beast is stirring deep in the Forest of Shadows – Mallix. Unless you can stop him, innocent lives will be lost."

Tom had no idea where the forest was, but there was sudden fire in his heart. "Show us the way," he said.

"It is many days' travel," Celesta said. "My horses will guide you." The two white stallions tossed their silver manes and raked the ground as if eager to leave at once. Celesta stepped gracefully from her chariot and gestured for Tom and Elenna to take her place.

Tom turned to Elenna. Her eyes

shone wide in the moonlight, but she nodded firmly. They straightened their backs and strode towards the ghostly vehicle. Tom stepped gingerly on to the translucent platform, half expecting his foot to go straight through; but though he could see the grass below, it felt firm. As Elenna climbed aboard, Tom took the reins, inhaling sharply at the icy burn of the leather in his hands.

"Thank you," he said to Celesta. "And farewell. We will not let you down." The ghostly warrior dipped her head, her dark eyes holding Tom's to the last as her form melted into the night.

Tom turned to the horses – a

perfectly matched pair, powerfully muscled and taller than any living steeds. He gave the cold reins a tug.

The two horses surged towards the cliff edge so fast Tom's stomach flipped. "Whoa!" He pulled on the reins, straining his muscles, trying to slow the phantom creatures, but they careered on, picking up more speed. Tom's heart shot into his mouth as they leapt out into the darkness. Elenna gasped, her knuckles white on the chariot's rim.

We're going to fall!

But instead of plummeting, the horses soared upwards, carrying them swiftly into the night sky. A fierce wind battered against Tom

and made Elenna's short hair whip
about her face. The impossible speed
tore at Tom's stomach. But his fear
quickly turned to breathless elation

as the stallions surged onwards, heading north. The landscape sped past in a dark blur below, villages no more than clusters of lights and rivers gleaming like silver snakes. Tom's heart filled with hope. As if in response, one of the stallions lifted his head and let out a joyful whinny, and the other followed suit as inky pastureland gave way to hills, steeped in shadow.

As they raced north beyond the mountains, a rolling darkness of tree-covered hills spread out below them – a mighty forest. The night sky changed too, mirroring the dusky landscape. Clouds billowed on the horizon, blocking out the stars, thickening to towering thunderheads. The horses tossed their manes and snorted, their ears flicked back in alarm, but they did not slow down. Wisps of vapour swept past, cold and cloying, thickening to a dense fog that swirled all around them. Before long, icy raindrops began to hit, pelting against Tom's skin like gravel. The horses ducked their heads against the driving rain, their long manes rippling out behind them. Tom gritted his teeth, frowning into the wind.

Lightning knifed through the sky, then again, flashing and flickering in every direction, making the clouds glow blue-white. The horses let out panicked screams. Tom yanked on the reins once more, trying to guide them lower, but with their eyes rolling, the shadow horses cantered on, faster than ever. Buffeted by the wind, the chariot pitched and rolled like a ship at sea. Tom clung to the reins, widening his stance. Elenna half-crouched beside him.

CRASH! Thunder echoed all around, a barrage of sound that went on and on. Another bolt of lightning seared past and thunder boomed again, so loud Tom felt as if his skull would split.

"We have to go lower, or we'll be struck!" Elenna cried, her voice barely reaching Tom over the wind.

"I can't control the horses!" Tom

shouted back. He lifted his shield with one arm, holding it over them both, just as another lightning strike crackled through the sky. *BOOM!*

It hit the wood of Tom's shield, throwing him hard against the rim of the chariot and leaving his shield smoking.

"Zargon has to be behind this!" Tom cried, thunder almost drowning out his words. Elenna clung to the chariot with both hands, her head ducked against the rain. Tom glanced at the horses. Their silver coats streamed with water and their muscles bunched with each frenzied step. *Surely we have to land soon!*

CRASH! Elenna let out a sharp cry and Tom's body jackknifed, his muscles cramping all at once as a bolt of lightning struck the chariot, sending a blaze of energy searing through him. *We've been hit!* The chariot rocked, then pitched sharply. Tom's stomach leapt. The horses, uncoupled from their harness, surged away, vanishing in another blinding flash of light. Tom made a grab for the rim of the chariot, but he could hardly feel his hands. The whole thing lurched again, then flipped over. Elenna screamed. Tom lost his grip and fell, plummeting through the wind and rain towards the treetops below.

1

THE FOREST OF SHADOWS

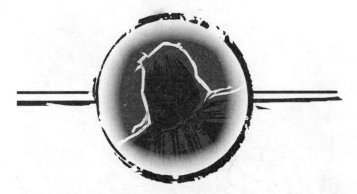

Jagged branches whipped past, snagging Tom's clothes, tearing at his flesh. A sharp pain slashed across his arm, then his cheek. Brittle cracks rang in his ears as boughs snapped beneath him. He braced himself for the landing just as the trees gave way and he crashed down into the undergrowth, springy foliage breaking his fall. With another thump, Elenna landed beside him.

Dazed and winded, Tom staggered up and took in the sudden, quiet darkness. A few heavy drops of rain pattered down around him, but the air was muggy and still. Crickets chirped to one another, hidden in the shadows.

"Are you all right?" he asked Elenna, his voice coming out as a croak. She groaned and pulled herself to her feet.

"I feel like I just fell out of the sky and hit every branch of a tree on the way down," she said. "But apart from that..." Elenna leaned suddenly towards him, her brow creased with concern. "Tom...look at your arm!"

Tom glanced down to see a long

tear in his tunic sleeve, showing a bloody gash underneath. Now the adrenaline from the fall was wearing off, he could feel the deep cut throbbing sharply. He took Epos's talon from his lightning-blackened shield. Its magical powers had healed many a grave injury in the past. But when he held it against his broken skin, expecting the edges of his cut to knit together, nothing happened. He flexed his fingers, wincing at the burning pain the movement caused.

"I think the lightning strike did something to my magic tokens," he told Elenna, trying to keep the pain and worry from his voice. She bit her lip, frowning.

"We can't leave that cut," she said, peering into the undergrowth. "There has to be something we can use…" A twig cracked somewhere in the darkness. A sudden explosion of wingbeats made Elenna jump as a hidden bird left its roost. Then silence returned. Tom shifted his shoulders, trying to ease the nagging feeling of unfriendly eyes watching them. Elenna shuddered. "But not here," she said. "We need to move. I'll collect herbs for a poultice as we go." She glanced about again, frowning hard. "Zargon could be anywhere!"

Tom sighed. Without any sort of guidance, or knowledge of the forest, they could wander aimlessly for days. They might never find the Evil Wizard, or the Beast called Mallix, at all...

Elenna led the way, scouring the ground as they went, occasionally bending stiffly to pick a sprig or leaf. Tom peered into the deep, velvety shadows all around them. He could barely see a thing in the dense foliage.

His arm throbbed, and each step felt like an immense effort to his bruised body, but he kept his senses alert for any sign of Zargon – or a Beast. The muggy air pressed against him, making it hard to breathe. Eventually, Tom heard the welcoming bubble of water ahead and quickened his pace. The trees parted, revealing a narrow, fast-flowing stream with mossy banks on either side.

"Let's stop and get that cut cleaned up," Elenna said.

Tom sank gratefully on to a moss-covered rock and rolled back his sleeve. He winced as Elenna gently bathed the cut with water, then packed the gash with crushed herbs. Lastly, she tore a strip from his ripped sleeve, and tied it over the wound. The cool, fresh herbs and the pressure of the bandage eased the pain almost at once.

"Thank you," Tom said. "Now, we'd better freshen up and fill our bottles. It might be a while before we find water again." His heart felt suddenly heavy at the thought of them wandering aimlessly in the dark forest. But they had little choice.

They both waded into the cold, shallow stream. Tom took a long drink, then splashed his face and neck, washing the dirt from his cuts and bruises. A branch snapped behind him. Tom spun, pulse racing, and stared into the trees.

Elenna let out a soft gasp. Tom turned back to see her stagger a few steps towards the bank then sink to her knees. A small dart was stuck in her neck. As he lunged towards her, she folded sideways, collapsing on to the riverbank, her eyes closed.

"Elenna!" Tom shook his friend, then felt a sharp pain in his thigh. He looked down. A dart was lodged in his own flesh. He plucked it free, then drew his sword and searched the shadows, but his vision doubled

and his legs almost buckled, rubbery and weak. He steadied himself on a branch and blinked, trying to focus, and ignore the nausea that was rising inside him. Slender figures loomed between the trunks. They wore some sort of dark, dull armour that almost seemed to blend with the trees, but their eyes shone in the dusky light. Tom squinted harder. A dim form leapt towards him, wielding a club, swinging for his head. Tom managed to lift his shield, but the blow sent it tumbling from his fingers.

"We mean you no harm!" he managed, but his words sounded slurred and strange. His tongue felt too big. As the armoured figure lifted

the club again, Tom raised his sword
and lunged but the forest swam
around him and he overbalanced,
blackness enveloping him before he
hit the ground.

1

CAPTIVES

Tom awoke to a swaying motion,
his ankles and wrists tugged above
him and his head lolling painfully.
Memory flooded back and he opened
his eyes, wincing at a sudden flicker
of torchlight in the darkness. He
wondered how long he'd been
unconscious. Two figures carried him
between them, bound to a pole by

his arms and legs. His captors were tall and slender, but muscular and with long straight hair. Now he was closer, Tom could see their armour was made from wooden plates etched with leaves and flowers. Elenna hung at his side, also tied to a pole,

her eyes bright in the firelight and
her teeth clenched with fury. More
people carrying torches walked on
either side of them, some dressed
in simple flowing gowns made of a
mossy material, others wearing the
carved wooden armour. They spoke

together in hushed, hurried voices,
and, although Tom didn't know their
language, he could hear the fear and
even anger in their tones. He spotted
a tall girl with sharp features and
chestnut hair holding his sword at
arm's length, inspecting it with a
look of horror. She said something
in her own language, then handed
the weapon to another in the group,
who dropped the sword into a sack
with a frown. Beyond them, a broad-
shouldered man was inspecting one of
Elenna's metal-tipped arrows, his lip
curled and his eyes fierce.

Tom shifted his arms and legs,
testing his bonds, but the ropes bit
deep into his flesh with no give in

them at all. He spotted more torches
ahead. A moment later, they were
carried into a clearing, bright with
firelight and surrounded by trees.
Wooden runways and platforms ran
between the tree canopies. Thatched
huts had been erected among many of
the branches – a whole treetop village,
with ropes and ladders leading up
from the ground. One of their captors
let out a cry. A moment later, people of
every age shimmied effortlessly down
the ladders and swarmed towards
them, their eyes wary.

An elder strode from the group. His
copper-coloured hair hung in braids,
and his eyes shone like amber in the
torchlight.

"Who are you, and why are you here?" he asked. The man's words were stilted and heavily accented – as if he rarely used the common tongue – but Tom could understand them. He felt a wave of relief. *Now we can explain!*

"Please free us from our bonds," Tom said, speaking slowly and clearly. "We come as friends." His head throbbed from being upside down, and his wrists and ankles burned.

The tall man's eyes narrowed. "Your weapons say otherwise," he said. "Such edged metal is not permitted in our forest – we honour nature here and accept only what the forest gives us. This protects the balance – something you clearly don't understand. You and

your companion must have come from a *city*." The man's face twisted with disgust on the last word.

"Yes!" Tom said. "We have been sent by Queen Aroha, from Pania."

He expected the name to be greeted with respect, or at least recognition. But instead, the man and the rest of the gathered people exchanged dark glances, muttering to one another under their breath.

"I am Lika," the man told him, touching the etched wooden plate on his chest. "I learned your words and ways from the traders that pass near to our home. We recognise no queen here. Only the law of the forest. We welcome friends, but you bring evil, forbidden weapons – and you have defiled our sacred spring." Lika scowled, his amber eyes sparking with fury.

"We meant no harm!" Elenna said.

"We were tired and thirsty. My friend is wounded, and I had to treat his arm."

"We are here to face a true enemy," Tom added. "An Evil Wizard called Zargon."

Lika turned and spoke to the gathered people, and Tom heard the name *Zargon* repeated back and forth, along with other words he didn't know.

With the torchlight in his eyes, Tom could only make out a few faces, but all wore the same hostile scowl. An older woman with greying hair pulled back from her face, and a green tunic of interwoven leaves, stepped forward and held a hand up for silence. Her hooded eyes, set over broad, high cheekbones, blazed with anger. She spoke a few sharp words to Lika – then she barked an order, jabbing a finger towards something on the ground. Tom twisted his neck painfully, and saw a wooden grille covering some kind of pit.

I don't like the look of that!

Two young men dragged the cover from the gaping hole. Another stepped in so close, Tom caught his smell of woodsmoke and herbs. The man took a wooden knife from his belt, and with two swift cuts, freed Tom from the pole. Tom slammed down on to his back, his limbs still bound together. Before he could

feel any relief – or even roll over –
calloused hands grabbed his arms
and legs and carried him roughly
towards the hole in the ground, then
heaved him inside. He splashed

down into thick, viscous mud at the bottom of a deep pit. A moment later, Elenna landed with a grunt beside him, splattering him with more mud. The grille that had covered the pit

crashed back into place.

Lika peered down at them through the grate, alongside the dark-haired woman. "We know of no 'Zargon'... but we know that you have defiled what we hold sacred. We know that you bring death and destruction to our home. To atone for your crimes, you will be buried now as our gift to the precious forest!"

RISING WATER

Wet mud sucked at Tom's body like quicksand. With his wrists and ankles still bound, he rolled first to his knees, then heaved himself clumsily to his feet. A rumbling sound echoed above him – something wooden was being dragged overhead. He looked up and could just make out some kind of chute through the

grid that closed them in. Elenna clambered up beside him. "We have to convince them we're on their side!" she said, just as a great spurt of water sloshed down over her face.

Elenna coughed and spluttered, staggering back as more water tumbled into the pit. Tom's feet sank deeper into the thick mud beneath them. Another chute slid into place, sending a second cascade splashing down beside the first.

Running his eyes over the pit's vertical sides, and the grate far above, Tom swallowed hard. *No way out!* The water was rising quickly, already creeping to his waist. He tugged at his bound wrists, drawing

on the magic of his golden breastplate
and heaving with all his strength,
but it felt like his bones would break
before the rope did. Through the
splash of the water he could just hear
the voices above them receding. Fear
quickened inside him as the torchlight
bobbed and faded.

"Come back!" he cried. "You can't
leave us like this!" The water inched
up his chest, then started climbing his
neck. He pushed up on to his toes, but
his feet sank deeper until he could
barely keep his chin above the water.
"Let us go!" he shouted, but he knew
that even if the villagers could hear
him over the gurgle of the water, only
Lika would understand his words.

Elenna growled in frustration, her head tipped right back, her airways only just above the surface. "This is ridiculous. We're their only hope of surviving whatever Zargon has planned, and they're going to drown us in this mud pit!" Then she raised her voice. "Come back!" she cried. "There's a Beast coming called Mallix! If you don't let us out to fight him, you'll all die!"

Tom heard voices, then made out a sudden flurry of movement. He felt a rush of hope which turned to alarm as Elenna gave a last muffled squeak, her mouth and nose going under. Her eyes glinted in the darkness, wide with panic. Tom clamped his own mouth shut to stop the water rushing in, then held his breath, his nostrils filling. The torchlight above wavered and burned brighter. Tom heard a grinding sound, and a scrape, then arguing voices... *Hurry up!* Tom's lungs burned, screaming for air. Suddenly, just as he felt he couldn't hold his breath an instant longer, the water stopped. The grate above was pulled away, and faces appeared, followed by hands. They gripped Tom and Elenna under the arms and tugged them, muddy and dripping, out of the pit and on to the ground.

Tom and Elenna lay gasping for breath and dripping wet, still bound at the ankles and wrists. Lika and the old woman glared down at them, while other villagers crowded close behind. Tom had never felt more helpless.

"What do you know of the dark spirit, Mallix?" Lika demanded.

Tom struggled up to a sitting position. "We're here to fight him," he said weakly. "Zargon plans to awaken the Beast. But Mallix won't be a spirit – he'll be flesh and blood and he'll destroy all in his path." Tom held Lika's angry gaze, then met the old woman's fierce glare. "You have to believe us!"

Lika turned to the older woman and spoke hurriedly in their own language. The woman looked down

at Tom and Elenna and spoke a few
sharp words, her dark gaze stern
and unyielding.

"Our shaman, Maya, does not
believe you," Lika said. "Maybe you

are trying to trick us into returning your weapons?"

Tom shook his head fiercely. "No! I am Avantia's Master of the Beasts, and it is my duty to defeat Evil. I promise you! I'll prove myself to you – there must be a way!"

Once again, Lika and Maya put their heads together. From Lika's quick hand movement and sidelong glances, Tom thought he was trying to persuade Maya to give them a chance. The woman's stern expression didn't change, but eventually, she nodded.

"There is one way," Lika told Tom. "A contest. A trial." He beckoned to someone among the gathered villagers, and a youth stepped forward. He was about Tom's age, but taller and with long red hair. He gazed down at Tom, clearly unimpressed by what he saw, and crossed arms over his armoured chest.

Tom shook his head. "I won't hurt someone with whom I have no quarrel!" he said.

"That is not our intention," Lika told him. "We will untie your bonds and you will follow us. But do not fight, or our poison darts will find you – and this time, they will be deadly."

Tom rubbed his smarting wrists as he and Elenna trudged in a procession through the forest. He wondered what possible contest they had in store for him. From the lightening sky, he guessed the sun would be rising soon, and a faint mist rose from the ground. Lika and Maya strode ahead of them, along with the tall boy who would challenge Tom. A pair of armoured warriors walked on either side, blowpipes ready in their hands. The rest of the village people followed behind – youths with drums, men and women carrying children, and sinewy elders with fierce bright eyes.

Before long, the procession halted in a clearing. Tom stopped and looked up in awe. A towering tree stood at the centre of a glade, its gnarled trunk and wide, spreading branches reaching far above the surrounding forest. Deep shadow nestled in the crook of each branch,

and despite the still air, the leaves
rustled like hushed voices – or like
rough scales slithering over wood.

"This tree is believed to have
grown from the blood of Mallix

himself," Lika said. "We come here
to honour the forest, and pray that
Mallix never returns. The challenge,
if you accept it, is to reach the
highest branch first. If the forest
accepts you – you will be able to beat
our champion climber."

Tom gazed up at the mighty tree
and suppressed a shiver. Its ancient
wood seemed to give off a strange
prickling energy, like the tense air
before a thunderstorm; but its wide
sturdy branches looked sound, with
plenty of hand and foot-holds.

He nodded. "I accept."

"Are you sure?" Elenna whispered.
"Your arm's badly hurt. And there's
something strange about that tree.

It's named for a Beast, after all. It could be a trap."

"I have to do it," Tom said, rubbing his bandaged arm and trying to sound bolder than he felt. "I've climbed hundreds of trees – and I can summon the powers of my magic armour if I need to." The red-haired youth gazed up into the branches and flexed his shoulders, clearly ready to go.

Tom felt a shiver of doubt – the boy was a head taller than him, and obviously used to climbing. But he swallowed his worries. *I have to win! Our lives depend on it.*

"Wish me luck!" he told Elenna, and stepped towards the tree.

MALLIX AWAKENS

As Tom reached up, setting his hand
on the rough bark of the great tree,
a drumbeat started up from the
gathered villagers – deep and even,
like the low thud of a heart. Tom's
opponent gazed at him, one eyebrow
arched, as if asking if he were ready.
Tom nodded. The youth gripped a
low bough, then vaulted upwards

and began to climb. Tom quickly followed suit. At first, the branches were broad and widely spaced. He had to reach far above his head to grip the bark and heave himself upwards, every muscle straining. His arms soon burned with the effort and his wound throbbed with each movement. Glancing at his opponent, Tom saw the taller boy had already pulled ahead, his greater reach giving him the advantage.

Tom scrambled to catch up, hauling himself on to the nearest bough, and then the next; but suddenly, he came to a gap. Grinding his jaw in frustration, he leapt for a lower bough, steadied himself, then started upwards again.

With his opponent now several branches above him, Tom pushed himself to climb faster than ever, ignoring the protest of his tired muscles and the pain in his injured arm, heaving himself on to each new bough and throwing caution to the wind. The drumbeat quickened below.

"Go, Tom!" came Elenna's call. "You can do it!"

I won't let her down. Tom reached for the next hold, then the next. The branches grew closer together higher in the tree, and he picked up speed, climbing hand over hand to the steady rhythm of the drum. He was

gaining on his opponent. His breath
came fast and heavy and sweat
trickled down his spine and across
his brow, but Tom didn't even pause
to wipe his stinging eyes.

The red-haired boy stopped for a
moment to shake the fatigue from
his arms. Tom quickly reached the
boy's level, then passed him. Hope
kindled in his chest as he made a
grab for the next bough, but he felt
a sudden wet heat as the wound
on his arm wrenched open, blood
welling under the bandage, and
he missed. Gasping in pain, Tom
scrambled for a hold with his other
hand, then slapped a forearm over
the branch. Straining every muscle,

he just managed to haul his chest
up, then pull the rest of his body
to safety. Looking up, light-headed
with effort, he saw the boy once more

above him, climbing swiftly.

Leaves soon blocked Tom's view of the ground, and his opponent's progress above was marked only by branches rustling and swaying in the dense canopy. Tom's breath came in ragged gasps. *I can't win.* Still, he put every shred of energy he had into the final leg of the climb, forcing his burning limbs to keep going; and suddenly, he emerged into daylight. The highest branch was in reach, silhouetted against the morning sky. The other boy stood tall, leaning against the tree trunk and smiling, victorious. Spread beneath them in the morning sun, the forest canopy reached as far as

Tom could see in every direction.

Tom sank back on to the lower branch, his energy spent and his heart heavy. *I've failed!* Above him, the other boy let out a cry of triumph, punching the sky. No one from below answered, and the boy looked confused. He called again, and there was no response.

A moment later, there were screams. Howls of terror filled the air. Tom's gut tightened with dread as the screams suddenly stopped, cut short all at once.

THUNK! The tree shuddered. The red-haired boy stumbled, his eyes widening with terror as he made a grab for the trunk, arms flailing.

He missed. Calling on the magical
strength of his golden breastplate,
Tom snatched the boy's wrist from
the air as he tumbled past. The
sudden weight almost overbalanced
him, but bracing himself, Tom

somehow pulled the boy to safety. The youth swallowed hard, then managed a shaky smile.

THUD! The sound rang hollowly from below them, and the boy's smile vanished. He and Tom exchanged a look of alarm as the tree shook from root to tip. Tom started to shimmy downwards, as fast as he could. The boy began to clamber down too.

"Elenna!" Tom cried. "What's happening?" Elenna didn't answer. Another *THUD!* rang out, and the constant whisper of the leaves became a tumult, as if a wind was lashing the branches. Panic rising, Tom half slid, half climbed down the tree until he was clear of the leaves. Horror gripped him as he took in the scene below. Zargon stood at the base of the tree, wielding a huge axe that glowed with a pale light of its own.

The stolen axe from the tomb in Pania, Tom realised, his belly churning with dread.

The wizard's sleeves were drawn back, exposing his muscular forearms, and his teeth were bared in a rictus of hate. A gaping cut, oozing with sap, yawned in the tree trunk, and as Tom watched, Zargon drew back his axe and sent it thudding deep into the heartwood once more. Beyond Zargon, the

villagers – and Elenna too – stood
frozen, surrounded by shimmering
purple light. Trapped by magic.

I have to stop him. But how?

With a high, whooping battle cry, the red-haired boy threw himself from the branches towards the wizard.

Zargon's gaze snapped upwards, cruel eyes narrowed to slits, and he lifted a hand. A bolt of purple energy struck the boy square in the chest, throwing him to the ground where he groaned, then lay still.

"I had hoped my storm would put a stop to your meddling!" Zargon called up to Tom. "But I like this better. Now you'll witness the rebirth of Mallix – if you survive the fall!" Zargon grinned, a hunter sure of his prey, then drew back his axe and with one final mighty strike, slammed it into the trunk, severing the ancient wood. *CREAK!* Tom's stomach lurched as the tree toppled – slowly at first, but gaining speed. With a mighty leap, Tom pushed off the wood, throwing himself as far as he could into the clearing, away from the falling tree. He landed in a crouch, splintering crashes of shattering wood and terrified screams echoing around him as people ran wildly in every direction, suddenly free of Zargon's spell.

Tom turned as the mighty tree smashed down through the canopy, snapping saplings like twigs beneath its vast weight and making the earth lurch. He scanned the wreckage

for Zargon, but the wizard had
vanished.

"Tom!" Elenna cried, reaching his
side and catching hold of his sleeve.
"Look!" She pointed at the fallen
tree. With a hideous, creaking groan,

the trunk split open along its length, revealing a viscous, glowing, purple sap.

Cries of fear and dismay went up from the villagers in the clearing as the sap boiled and bulged, forming into a long, glistening scaled shape – a snake, but thicker across than a man's chest and glowing all the sickly colours of putrid, rotting flesh – purples, yellows and greens.

Mallix!

DOUBLE TROUBLE

The glowing creature inside the tree
coiled and twisted, breaking free of
the wood with splinters and pops,
its bruise-coloured flesh dripping
with slime. Elenna gasped as Mallix
rose up, revealing the flat, hooded
skull of a cobra, and huge luminous
eyes. The stench of rotting offal hit
Tom like a blow, almost making him

gag. He reached instinctively for his sword, then cursed. *I can't fight Mallix bare-handed!*

Glancing over his shoulder, Tom saw the villagers backing slowly away, wide-eyed with shock. Maya was at the front of the group, her strong, stern features clouded with uncertainty as she took in the sight of the rising Beast. Lika stood at her side, shaking his head slowly, his mouth hanging open.

"Run!" Tom cried. Lika glanced at him and blinked. "Tell them all to flee!" Tom shouted. "This isn't a tree spirit – it's a Beast!" As if to prove Tom's words, Mallix let out an angry hiss, a forked tongue flickering

from between his lips. Tom turned to see the snake's jaws stretch wide, revealing long pale fangs, dripping with dark venom. Tom snatched up a fallen branch, wielding it like a club. Elenna did the same, just as the snake shot two streams of poison from its fangs over their heads and into the clearing. Tom spun to see the poison strike Maya in the chest. *No!* His heart clenched and the woman's eyes widened in shock, the venom spreading rapidly over her clothes and skin, hardening into a rough, dark crust, freezing her to the spot. *Tree bark!* Tom realised as the dark layer closed over Maya's terrified face. *She's been turned to wood!*

Lika stared at Maya, his face draining of all colour, then turned to Tom and Elenna.

"Take these!" he cried, reaching into a large satchel on his back, drawing out first Tom's sword and shield, then Elenna's bow and arrows. As Tom raced forward to take his weapons, a piercing scream split the air. He turned to see Mallix shoot another stream of venom at a woman holding a small child. Elenna bundled the villager and her baby aside. The venom struck the ground, fizzing away where it had hit, right where they had been standing.

Tom turned back to the Beast. Mallix's head swayed gently from side to side as he gazed out over the clearing, his wide eyes taking in all the people within reach. More venom was already dripping from the Beast's fangs.

Tom put a hand to the red jewel in his belt. "Leave these innocent people alone. They are unarmed and cannot fight. I am Master of the Beasts! Fight me!"

Mallix's unblinking eyes swivelled towards Tom and a forked tongue flickered from between his fangs. *Hssssss!* The sound was filled with a cold menace that made Tom's skin crawl, but he lunged for the snake with the speed of his magical leg armour, hacking for Mallix's slimy flesh. Almost too quickly to register, the snake recoiled, darting out of range.

Holding Mallix's steady gaze, Tom called on the power of the red jewel in his belt to communicate once more. "Coward!" he spat, putting all the contempt he could muster into the word, and backing into the vegetation. Mallix slithered onwards, his pale eyes never leaving Tom's face. Tom drew a breath of relief as the sounds from the clearing receded. But then his foot hit a tree stump behind him and he half stumbled. With a hiss, Mallix struck out, his fangs snapping for Tom's throat. Tom threw up his shield, his arm almost buckling as the Beast's fangs thudded into the wood. He wrenched his shield from the Beast's teeth.

"Is that the best you can do?" Tom

taunted, stepping around the stump. Mallix rose up again, his dark pupils widening as he watched Tom hungrily. Backing further into the forest, Tom lifted his sword, and smiled. "Come on. I'm waiting!"

With a hiss of rage, Mallix sent a spurt of venom shooting towards Tom. Tom dived and rolled to dodge the poison, then leapt to his feet. Another deadly jet was heading right for his head. Tom caught it on the wood of his shield and sank into a crouch, ready for the next strike.

Jaws open, Mallix lunged. Combining the magical speed of his leg armour with the sword skills of his gauntlets, Tom dodged sideways,

swinging his blade in a shimmering
arc.

THWACK! His sword sliced cleanly
through the Beast's flesh, severing
its head. Tom sagged with relief as
the snake's body writhed in agony,

dark blood gushing from the severed
stump. But then he gaped, horrified,
as four new heads formed within
the wound in the creature's neck,
writhing as if fighting for space. As
Tom staggered backwards in shock,

he saw them fight their way clear of the wound, stretching and rising and looming above him...

Now *eight* glowing eyes were watching him with seething hatred, while four tongues flickered and

hissed in rage. Mallix's many mouths snapped open, all of them ready to strike.

Tom didn't know which way to leap.

SNAKE PIT

Poised on the balls of his feet, Tom watched Mallix's heads intently, not even daring to blink. One head whipped towards him. Tom ducked sideways and threw up his shield, smashing it into the creature's blunt nose. From the corner of his eye, he saw a second head darting though the air, fangs bared. Tom swiped

with his sword, but the angle was
all wrong and his blade glanced off
the creature's scales. Wincing, Tom
braced himself, expecting to feel the
agony of sharp, deadly teeth...

THUNK! Mallix recoiled with

a hiss, his empty fangs snapping shut, an arrow jutting from one pale eye. Writhing with agony, the Beast twisted around and darted away through the trees.

Elenna appeared at Tom's side.

"Thanks!" he said, his knees suddenly weak. "You were just in time!"

Elenna fitted another arrow to her bow. "Sorry I wasn't faster," she said. "I've been talking with the villagers. I told Lika to lead them home, to safety... But now it looks like that was a mistake!"

Tom followed the direction of Elenna's gaze and saw she was right. Mallix was heading back

in the direction they had come –
straight towards the village.

"We'd better hurry!" he said, then
set off at a run.

Elenna kept pace at his side,
leaping over tree roots and heaps
of fallen leaves. "I had hoped that
arrow might finish Mallix off!" she
said. "But it hardly seemed to slow
him down at all!"

"I don't think we can defeat him
with weapons," Tom panted. "I cut
off his head – but you saw how that
ended."

"Badly," Elenna agreed. "So,
what's the plan?"

"Maybe we need to disable him
somehow, like we did Teknos?" Tom

answered. But there was no pulley system at the village – and Mallix was much faster than Teknos had been. Tom wracked his brains, trying to come up with a solution, but the sound of terrified screams from ahead suddenly drove all other thoughts from his mind. He and Elenna put on a burst of speed and hurtled into the clearing.

Mallix was coiled in the centre of the village with heads reared high, while armoured villagers tried to strike him with clubs. The Beast spat venom from his jaws while swiftly ducking every blow, his long tail swiping at his attackers. Many brave warriors had already been turned to wood mid-fight, their faces etched with terror. Most of the youngest and oldest villagers had found shelter in their treetop houses and were throwing pots and pans, and whatever else they could find down at the Beast. But nothing seemed to slow Mallix, not even the arrow sticking out of one of his eyes. The snake's four heads darted this way and that, shooting venom at anyone within reach.

Tom scanned the clearing and spotted the pit he and Elenna had been thrown into, still open and half filled with mud.

"Cover me!" he told Elenna. She fitted an arrow to her bow and aimed it at the raging Beast, while Tom stepped in front of the pit, and lifted his sword.

"Mallix!" Tom cried. "I've cut off one head – I can cut off four more. Turn and fight, you stinking worm!"

The Beast's heads swivelled towards Tom at once, his seven good eyes bulging with fury. Tom grinned and waved his sword.

"What are you waiting for, you rotting, putrid pile of flesh?" he called. Mallix surged forward with a hiss, knocking his attackers flying. All his hideous mouths opened wide, spitting arcs of venom. Tom ducked behind his shield, feeling the poison splatter the wood, waiting for just the right moment...

As soon as Mallix's slimy body came within reach, Tom slammed his shield upwards into one scaled jaw, and the hilt of his sword into another. Then, throwing down his weapons, Tom summoned the strength of his golden breastplate, grabbed the Beast with both arms and dived backwards, wrenching Mallix with him into the pit.

Mud filled Tom's nose and eyes as he plunged into darkness, feeling the Beast's slimy, muscular flesh wrap around his body and squeeze tight. Twisting and stretching his neck, Tom managed to break the surface of the mud, gasping for air,

but the Beast still held him tight. He
heaved himself free of one slippery
coil only for another to clamp
around his ribs. The revolting stench
of Mallix up close made Tom's head
swim. He hammered with his fists

on the stinking flesh, twisting and heaving to get free. Mallix tightened his grip on Tom's chest, forcing the breath from his lungs.

"Tom!" Elenna called, her voice high and panicked. "I can't find a mark! I might hit you!"

Tom's lungs shuddered with lack of air. He realised he had one weapon left. Fighting against his revulsion, Tom bent his head to the slimy snake coiled about his body, called on the strength of heart of his golden chainmail, and bit deep into the scales. The flesh gave with a hideous crunch and hot blood welled in Tom's mouth. Mallix's stranglehold went slack, just for an instant – but it was long enough for Tom to scramble free. Elenna and Lika both reached into the pit, grabbed his arms and pulled him up.

A pair of armoured villagers, ready with the lid of the pit, heaved it into place. Others started to hammer stakes through the wooden slats, pinning it to the ground.

With Mallix trapped, Tom gagged and spat, wiping his mouth clean, then retrieved his sword and shield. All around him, exhausted warriors sagged to the ground. Some started to chip away the layer of bark from their comrades. To Tom's relief, they uncovered living, breathing people underneath.

Tom and Elenna exchanged a weary smile – but suddenly, a mighty crash snatched away any thoughts of victory. Tom spun as Mallix burst out through the wooden grate and surged upwards, dripping with mud and slime. The Beast's seven good eyes blazed with fury, and his jaws yawned wide, venomous fangs ready to strike.

THE QUEST CONTINUES

Tom snatched up his sword and shield as Elenna aimed her bow. *Whoosh!* Her arrow sank deep into Mallix's flesh. The four-headed snake hissed in fury, then shot up a nearby trunk into the treetop village. Eyes rolling madly, Mallix struck out wildly with his tail. Wood

cracked and splintered. Terrified
men and women with children
on their backs fled their homes,
hurrying down ladders and into
the forest. Elenna fired another
arrow, but it only seemed to make
the Beast's attack more frenzied.
Broken timbers rained down. A
young warrior with a blowpipe
hanging from her belt darted past
Tom. Struck with a sudden idea, he
grabbed her arm.

"Wait!" he said. As she turned
towards to him, eyes glazed with
terror, Tom pointed to the blowpipe
at her side. "The poison," Tom said.
"Have you got more?" The woman's
gaze snapped into focus. She looked

down at the pipe, then at Tom, understanding kindling in her eyes. She nodded and pointed towards a gourd hanging from a nearby tree. Tom raced towards it, and looked inside. A white and viscous sap filled the vessel.

Elenna reached Tom's side in an instant. "It's worth a try!" she said. Tom poured white gloop over the blade of his sword, and Elenna hurriedly dipped her arrows. They exchanged a grim-faced nod, then turned back to the Beast.

Mallix hung from a tree now, showering venom over the villagers running for their lives. Tom leapt towards the snake, using his shield to block the venom and swinging his sword, just as Elenna let her first poisoned arrow fly.

THUNK! The arrow struck Mallix right between one set of bulging eyes. Tom raked his blade across scaled flesh, then darted back out of reach.

The snake dropped down from his perch and reared up in front of Tom and Elenna, forked tongues flickering. Tom lunged, slashing with his sword, finding a mark. With a hiss, the Beast turned all his heads towards him. Tom struck again. Another of Elenna's arrows plunged deep into Mallix's scales. But the snake hardly seemed to register the poisoned wounds.

It's not working! Desperation seized Tom's heart. Leaping forward, he managed to land another fleeting blow on Mallix's flesh.

Writhing with fury, the Beast shot a spurt of venom towards Tom. Tom ducked and blocked with his shield, but in the same instant, Mallix sent his tail whipping through the air. Tom sliced for it with his sword, but the tail swept onwards, coiling around Tom's waist and squeezing hard. Tom gasped, all the breath forced from his body at once. His sword and shield tumbled from his weakened grip. Flashing points of light crowded his vision. He felt a thud as Elenna fired another arrow into Mallix's coils. With a rasping hiss, the Beast turned and spat a gobbet of venom over her before she could aim again. Tom watched in horror as tree bark covered his friend – closing over her panicked face last of all. The Beast swivelled his many pale eyes downwards, and Tom found himself staring back into Mallix's cruel gaze, helpless and breathless, unable to move.

I've killed one Master of the Beasts, Mallix hissed in Tom's mind. *Though you have fought valiantly, I will kill you too!* The Beast's coils tightened again, and Tom felt bile rise into his throat, the pain in his ribs almost blinding him. But still, he held the Beast's gaze – and saw the pupils dilate then narrow. The snake shook his heads, as if suddenly groggy, and Tom felt the pressure about his chest lessen, just a fraction. *The poison is working!* Hope flared inside him. *If I can just hold on...*

One of Mallix's heads swayed, the pale eyes clouding over. Tom's whole body shook with agony and lack of air, and he felt his last strength ebbing away. The final, kind release of death beckoned, but he forced himself to bear the pain – to stay awake.

Mallix's other heads began to dip as well, his eyes opening and closing. Then suddenly, the grip of the scaly flesh was gone and Tom tumbled free. He fell to the earth, retching and gasping for breath, as the snake lurched from side to side. Tom staggered up as the Beast's body sank to the ground. A soft rush

of breath, almost like a sigh, hissed
from between the snake's four sets
of jaws.

Tom reached for the red jewel
in his belt as he approached with
caution. "Rest now," he told Mallix.
"Be free from Zargon's evil, and
slumber once more." Reaching out,
he put a hand on one of the snake's
ridged brows.

Resssst, the Beast repeated.
*Yessss...I remember now... I was
sssssleeping... Thank you...Master
of the Beasssts...* And with another
gentle sigh, Mallix's huge body
changed colour, turning from
slimy purple and yellow, to glossy
greenish brown.

Villagers crowded closer around Tom and the sleeping Beast, many wielding torches. Lika stepped to Tom's side and clapped a hand on his shoulder. "We should burn what remains, in case that unnatural thing returns," Lika said.

Tom shook his head. "Mallix is no longer driven by Evil. He is defenceless now." As Tom spoke, the Beast's body shimmered like moonlight reflected in water, then blurred. Tom blinked and refocussed his eyes – but the light had gone, and only a lacy white snakeskin remained where the Beast's body had lain. The villagers stared at it with awe.

"We owe you a debt of thanks," Lika told Tom. "And an apology."

Tom shook his head, taking in the wooden living statues all around him, the broken ladders and shattered homes in the treetops above. "It is my job to defeat Beasts," he said. "But you will need help to free all your people and rebuild. Elenna and I could stay for a while."

It was Lika's turn to shake his head. "I think it more pressing you find the wizard that started all of this, before he unleashes more Evil on this land."

Tom nodded. "You are right. But first, I need to help my friend."

With Lika at his side, it didn't take Tom long to free Elenna from her tree-bark prison. She threw her arms around his neck as soon as she could and held tight. "I thought you really were dead this time!" she

cried. "And I couldn't do anything!"

Lika gave Tom and Elenna a parcel of bread and edible roots for the journey ahead and helped to rebind Tom's injured arm. Once they were ready, Lika fetched the tall boy who had challenged Tom to climb.

"Jed will show you the quickest way out of the forest," Lika said. The red-haired boy smiled and beckoned for Tom and Elenna to follow.

"Ready?" Tom asked Elenna. Every inch of his body ached, weighed down by a weariness like never before, and he couldn't remember the last time he'd slept. Elenna looked as bad as Tom felt – pale and pinched, with dark circles under her eyes. But she nodded and flashed him a grin.

"Of course!" she said. "We've got a Quest to complete – and while Zargon's on the loose, I'm not going to give up!"

Tom returned Elenna's grin, and, slowly, painfully, they both set off after Jed, into the strengthening light of a new day.

THE END

CONGRATULATIONS, YOU HAVE COMPLETED THIS QUEST!

At the end of each chapter you were awarded a special gold coin.
The QUEST in this book was worth an amazing 8 coins.

Look at the Beast Quest totem picture opposite to see how far you've come in your journey to become

MASTER OF THE BEASTS.

The more books you read, the more coins you will collect!

Do you want your own
Beast Quest Totem?

1. Cut out and collect the coin below
2. Go to the Beast Quest website
3. Download and print out your totem
4. Add your coin to the totem

www.beastquest.co.uk

8

READ THE BOOKS, COLLECT THE COINS!
EARN COINS FOR EVERY CHAPTER YOU READ!

550+ COINS
MASTER OF THE BEASTS

410 COINS
HERO

350 COINS
WARRIOR

230 COINS
KNIGHT

180 COINS
SQUIRE

44 COINS
PAGE

8 COINS
APPRENTICE

550+
515
480
445
410
395
380
365
350
320
290
260
230
217
206
191
180
112
76
44
30
19
8

READ ALL THE BOOKS IN SERIES 26:
THE FOUR MASTERS!

TEKNOS
THE OCEAN CRAWLER

MALLIX
THE SILENT STALKER

SILEXA
THE STONE CAT

KYRON
LORD OF FIRE

Don't miss the next exciting Beast Quest book: SILEXA, THE STONE CAT!

Read on for a sneak peek...

FALLEN HERO

Tom and Elenna skirted around a thorn bush then ducked under a hanging loop of vine. They were following their guide, Jed, through the forest. Tom ached all over. A gash on his arm, which he'd received falling from a flying chariot, itched and throbbed under its makeshift bandage. Elenna looked grey with exhaustion and her breathing sounded heavy in the muggy air.

Since they had begun their Quest to retrieve four powerful ancient weapons from the Evil Wizard Zargon, neither of them had slept. Zargon had stolen the weapons from the crypts beneath Queen Aroha's palace, and each was capable of waking an ancient Beast. Tom and Elenna had already defeated two such fearsome creatures – the latest a giant, many-headed snake called Mallix. And, although he and Elenna were both battered and ready to drop with weariness, Tom knew they couldn't rest. Zargon would do everything in his power to unleash the final two Beasts, and there was no telling what death and havoc they would wreak.

Jed, a tall young forest-dweller with long red hair and engraved wooden armour, stopped and looked back, waiting for them to catch up. Jed didn't speak the common tongue, but he had become friends with Tom and Elenna since they saved his treetop village from Mallix's attack.

As Tom reached Jed's side, the boy lowered one hand palm downwards, signalling that they should rest. Tom sank gratefully on to a nearby tree stump and Elenna sat beside him.

"We can't be far from the edge of the forest now," Tom said.

Elenna nodded, then let out a sigh. Jed would soon return home to his village, but Tom and Elenna's journey was far from over. "If only we had some idea of where Zargon is headed," she said.

As Tom thought of the Evil Wizard's ability to transport himself at will, frustration welled inside him. "He could be anywhere in Tangala by now!"

"We have found him twice before. We'll find him again," Elenna said, but looking at her weary, grime-streaked face, Tom could see she wasn't convinced.

Suddenly, he heard a soft whickering sound through the trees. *A horse?*

Elenna turned her head, listening, while Jed's eyes widened in alarm.

"Do you think that could be Zargon?" Elenna whispered.

Beckoning for Jed to follow, Tom and Elenna set off in search of the horse. Their guide looked pale and anxious, freezing when the distant creature let out a snort.

He's probably never seen a horse, Tom realised. "Don't be afraid," he said, hoping to reassure the boy with his tone. Jed still looked uneasy, but he nodded and started off again.

Before long, the trees parted,

revealing a small, grassy glade. Jed gasped at the sight of the chestnut mare standing at the centre. The horse was saddled and armoured, ready for battle. Her red-brown coat and black tail shone as if just brushed, and her silver armour glinted in the sun. A mossy white stone jutted from the grass at her feet. Tom could just make out some writing carved into it as he slowly moved towards the beautiful horse. "Hello...what are you doing here?" he murmured. The horse lifted her head, watching him from huge, gentle eyes. Tom reached for her bridle, but to his surprise, his hand went straight through the leather. The horse whinnied and shied away, her form suddenly shadowy and transparent. She broke into a canter and quickly disappeared into the trees.

Some sort of vision? Tom wondered. *A phantom?*

"Na! Neala!" Jed hissed. The boy was staring at the space where the horse had been.

"It's all right," Tom said, but Jed shook his head fiercely, then turned and sprinted away into the forest.

Elenna frowned and pointed to the white stone. "It looks like a grave marker," she said.

Tom bent and scraped away the moss that covered the writing. "'Here lies Roger'," he read aloud. "He must be buried here. I wonder who he was…"

"*I* am Roger," said a low, hollow voice. Tom turned to see a tall, armoured man step from the treeline. Pulse racing, Tom reached for the hilt of his sword. The stranger seemed maybe twenty years of age, with a sparse, neatly trimmed dark beard and grey eyes. As Roger turned and let out a whistle, Tom noticed with a sudden chill that he could see right through the warrior's frame. The soft thud of hooves answered Roger's whistle, and a moment later, the armoured mare trotted to his side. Roger smiled and stroked her glossy mane as she nuzzled his shoulder. "This is Windspur," Roger told Tom and Elenna. "She's rather nervous of strangers. Although, from your shield, I think you must be a Master of the Beasts?"

"I am," Tom said, bowing his head.

Read
SILEXA, THE STONE CAT
to find out what happens next!

Find out more about the NEW mobile game at
www.beast-quest.com

Meet three new heroes with the power to tame the Beasts!